## WITHDRAWN

Damaged, Obsolete, or Surplus
Jackson County Library Services

12/00

**JACKSON
COUNTY**
*Library Services*

**HEADQUARTERS**
**413 West Main Street**
**Medford, Oregon 97501**

# HOLLY KELLER

# Geraldine and Mrs. Duffy

Greenwillow Books

*An Imprint of HarperCollinsPublishers*

# FOR JESSE

Black line and watercolor paints
were used for the full-color art.
The text type is Geometric 706 BT.
Geraldine and Mrs. Duffy
Printed in Hong Kong by South China
Printing Company (1988) Ltd.
www.harperchildrens.com

Keller, Holly.
Geraldine and Mrs. Duffy / by Holly Keller.
    p.   cm.
"Greenwillow Books."
Summary: Geraldine and her little
brother Willy try to pull pranks on
their new babysitter.
ISBN 0-688-16887-6 (trade)
ISBN 0-688-16888-4 (lib. bdg.)
[1. Babysitters—Fiction.   2. Brothers and
sisters—Fiction.   3. Pigs—Fiction.]
I. Title.   PZ7.K28132Gab   2000
[E]—dc21   99-16215   CIP

1 2 3 4 5 6 7 8 9 10 First Edition

"**W**e don't want a new baby-sitter to stay with us,"
Geraldine said when Mama went to let Mrs. Duffy in.
"Why not?" Mama asked.
"Because we don't know her," Willy said,
"and besides, I'm not a baby."

Mama gave Mrs. Duffy some instructions,
then she kissed Geraldine and Willy good-bye.
"Behave, you two," she said.

The minute Mama was out the door,
Willy started to cry.
Geraldine made a face.
"Willy IS a baby," she told Mrs. Duffy,
and she marched off to her room.

"My, my, my," said Mrs. Duffy,
and she tried to pick Willy up.
Willy grabbed the table and wouldn't let go.
"Would you like a peppermint candy, Willy?"
Mrs. Duffy asked. "I have some in my pocket."

"No," Willy cried, and he ran into the coat closet.
He slammed the door shut behind him.
Geraldine came back.
"Can I have a peppermint?" she asked.
"Pink or green?" asked Mrs. Duffy.
"Pink," said Geraldine, and she popped it
into her mouth.

"I want green," Willy shouted from inside the closet,
 and he tried to open the door.
"Help!" he yelled. "I'm stuck!"
"No, you aren't," said Geraldine,
 and she turned the doorknob.
The door opened, and Willy came flying out.

"My, my, my," Mrs. Duffy said again,
and she gave Willy his candy.
Then she checked her watch
and said it was time for a bath.
"No," Willy said. "I'm not dirty.
Look!"

"I can get Willy into the tub," said Geraldine.
"No, you can't," said Willy, and he threw himself
into the wastepaper basket.

"Okay," Geraldine whispered to Willy.
"Then I'll play with Jerome myself."
"What do you mean?" asked Willy.
"I'm not telling," said Geraldine,
and she disappeared.

"I'm ready for my bath," Willy said.
He pulled himself out of the basket.
"Good, good, good," said Mrs. Duffy,
and she patted Willy on the head.
"When you're all clean, we'll have
some milk and cookies."

Willy went to see what Geraldine
was doing with Jerome.
"Sssshhhh," said Geraldine.
"Let's not tell Mrs. Duffy yet."

When there was a little water in the tub,
Geraldine turned off the faucet.
"That's not enough water, Geraldine,"
said Mrs. Duffy.
"We like it that way, don't we, Willy?"
Geraldine said.
"We like it that way," Willy echoed.

Mrs. Duffy went to get their pajamas,
and Geraldine put Jerome into the tub.
Then she and Willy climbed in too.
"Well, well, well," said Mrs. Duffy. "How nice."
Willy tried not to laugh.

"Oh, dear, dear, dear!" Mrs. Duffy gasped
when she finally noticed Jerome paddling
around in the water.
"Take him out this minute! Now, now, now!"
Geraldine grabbed Jerome and put him on
the bathroom floor.
"Not there!" screeched Mrs. Duffy.
And Jerome zipped out the door.

Geraldine climbed out of the tub
and ran after him.
Willy ran after Geraldine.

Mrs. Duffy ran too.

But Jerome was gone.

Geraldine looked under the chairs.

Willy looked behind the curtains.

Mrs. Duffy looked in the closets.

Nobody found him.

"I was only trying to be helpful," said Geraldine.
"What if we never find him?" Willy cried.
"Oh, no, no, no," groaned Mrs. Duffy,
    and she put an ice pack on her head.

Then all of a sudden Geraldine saw Jerome.

"There he is!" shouted Geraldine.

"There he is!" shouted Willy.

"Where, where, where?" demanded Mrs. Duffy.

Geraldine and Willy pointed.

"Don't move," said Mrs. Duffy, and she
climbed up onto the table.
She edged carefully toward the bookcase.
The table started to wobble,
and the vase of flowers shook.
"Look out!" she roared suddenly,
and she lunged for Jerome.

"Yay!" shouted Geraldine.
"Yay!" shouted Willy.
"Oh, oh, oh," said Mrs. Duffy,
and Geraldine put Jerome
back into his tank.

Mrs. Duffy started to laugh.

"Do you think you two are ready for bed now?"
she asked.

"Milk and cookies first," said Geraldine and Willy.

"Right, right, right," said Mrs. Duffy.

"Milk and cookies first."

"You're a nice baby-sitter," said Geraldine
when Mrs. Duffy tucked them into bed.
"Will you come again soon?" Willy asked.
Mrs. Duffy kissed them good night.
"Yes, yes, yes," she said.

And when Mama
came home
at ten o'clock,
everyone was
fast, fast, fast
asleep.